# The
# Story Girl
### Book 2 ™

From the author of Anne of Green Gables

# L.M. Montgomery

# 'The Story Girl

**Book 2**

# MEASLES, MISCHIEF, AND MISHAPS

*Adapted by Barbara Davoll*

Zonder**kidz**

# Zonder**kidz**.

*The children's group of Zondervan*

www.zonderkidz.com

*Measles, Mischief, and Mishaps*
© 2004 The Zondervan Corporation, David Macdonald, trustee and
Ruth Macdonald

Requests for information should be addressed to:
Grand Rapids, Michigan 49530

*Editor: Gwen Ellis*
*Interior design: Susan Ambs*
*Art direction: Laura Maitner*

04 05 06 07 /❖OP/ 10 9 8 7 6 5 4 3 2 1

# Contents

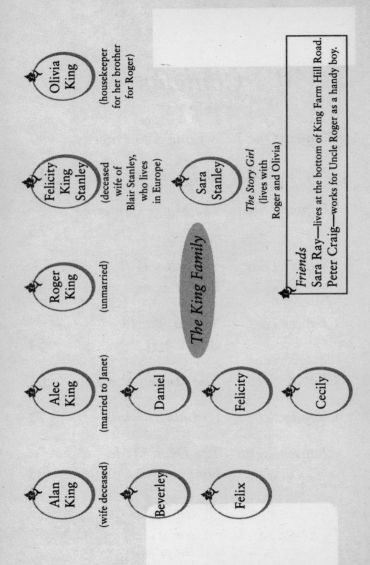

The King Family

Olivia King (housekeeper for her brother for Roger)

Felicity King Stanley (deceased wife of Blair Stanley, who lives in Europe)

Sara Stanley — *The Story Girl* (lives with Roger and Olivia)

Roger King (unmarried)

Alec King (married to Janet)

Daniel

Felicity

Cecily

Alan King (wife deceased)

Beverley

Felix

**Friends**
Sara Ray — lives at the bottom of King Farm Hill Road.
Peter Craig — works for Uncle Roger as a handy boy.

# A Long Ago Tragedy

*"There are things one just knows about,"*
*said the Story Girl with dignity.*
*"One feels about them."*

# Chapter One

There is no way to explain the fun we had on Prince Edward Island that summer. My brother, Felix, and I had always been lonely living with just father in Toronto. We had never had the joy of having lots of friends, but all that summer there was a whole gang of cousins to argue and play with.

Of all of the King cousins, I guess our favorite was who we called the Story Girl, Sara Stanley. A bond formed between us. Maybe because she, like us, didn't have a mother who was living. We understood her so well, and she understood us. During the previous week, she had been away visiting Aunt Louisa in Charlottetown, and we had been missing her and her funny stories. But now she was back and life was good again.

The day she came back to us, she was wearing a wreath of flowers she called Canterbury Bells in her hair. Her eyes were unusually pretty, though she was not as pretty as Felicity or even as lovely as our cousin Cecily. It just seemed Sara had a fresh beauty that gave her a sparkle the other girls didn't have.

And the Canterbury Bells in her hair almost made her seem like a princess.

She said, "Isn't Canterbury Bells a lovely name for a flower? It makes you think of cathedrals and chimes. Let's go over to Uncle Stephen's Walk in the orchard. I heard a story while I was gone—a *true* story—about an old lady I saw in town at Aunt Louisa's. She was such a dear old lady with lovely silvery curls." Once again, we were held captive by her voice and were soon carried away by the story she told.

"My story is about Mrs. Dunbar and the captain of the *Fanny*," she said, sitting down and leaning against a tree trunk. "It's sad and beautiful and true. I do love to tell stories that I know really happened. Mrs. Dunbar lives next door to Aunt Louisa in town. She is so sweet. You wouldn't think to look at her that she had ever had a tragedy in her life, but she has. Aunt Louisa told me that it happened long, long ago. Doesn't it seem that interesting things like this always took place long ago? They never seem to happen at the present. Well, anyway, it happened in 1849. Like folks from many places, a number of young men from our Island got the "gold fever" and took off for the gold fields of California, hoping to become rich.

"It's easy to go to California now, but it was a very different matter back then. There were no railroads, as there are now. If you wanted to go to California, you had to go in a sailing vessel all the way around Cape Horn. It was a long and dangerous journey. Sometimes it took more than six months. When you got there, you had no way of sending word back home except by the same way you had just come. It sometimes took more than a year before people at home heard a word about you. Can you imagine how difficult that would be?

"But these young men didn't think of things like that. All they could think about were riches and gold. They made their arrangements and chartered a sailing vessel, the *Fanny,* to take them to California.

"The captain of the *Fanny* is the hero of my story. His name was Alan Dunbar, and he was young and handsome. Heroes always are, you know. Aunt Louisa said he was in love—wildly in love—with Margaret Grant. Margaret was as beautiful as a dream, with soft blue eyes and clouds of golden hair. And she loved Alan Dunbar just as much as he loved her. But her parents were bitterly opposed to him. They forbade Margaret to see or speak to him. They hadn't anything against him as a man; they just didn't want her to waste her life by marrying a sailor.

"Well, when Alan Dunbar learned that he would be going to California on the *Fanny,* he was in despair. He felt he could *never* go so far away for so long and leave his Margaret behind. And Margaret felt she could never let him go. I know *exactly* how she felt."

"How can you know?" interrupted Peter suddenly. "You ain't old enough to have a boyfriend. How can you know?"

The Story Girl looked at Peter with a frown. She didn't like to be interrupted when telling a story.

"There are things one *just knows* about," said the Story Girl with dignity. "One *feels* about them."

Peter was quiet but not convinced. The Story Girl continued.

"Finally, Margaret ran away with Alan, and they were married in Charlottetown. Alan intended to take her with him to California on the *Fanny*. If it was a hard journey for a man, it would be even more difficult for a woman. But Margaret would have dared anything for Alan's sake.

"They spent three days of happiness before receiving the bad news. The crew and passengers of the *Fanny* refused to let Captain Dunbar take his wife along. Margaret would have to stay behind. All of his pleading and prayers did no good. They say Alan stood on the deck of the *Fanny* and begged the men while the tears ran down his face; but they would not listen. He had to leave Margaret behind. Oh, what a sad parting it must have been!"

There was heartbreak in the Story Girl's voice and tears came into our eyes. There in the orchard, we cried over a story that had happened many years before.

"When it was all over, Margaret's mother and father forgave her for marrying Alan, and she went back home to *wait*. And *wait*. How awful the *waiting* must have been for her. Almost a year later, a letter finally arrived—but not from Alan. Alan was dead. Though the letter did not reveal how Alan died, it did say that he had been buried in California. While Margaret had been thinking of him, longing for him, and praying for him, he lay unknowing in his lonely, faraway grave."

Cecily jumped up, shaking with sobs. "Oh, don't . . . don't go on," she begged. "I can't bear to hear any more."

"There is no more," said the Story Girl. "That was the end of it—the end of everything for Margaret. It didn't kill her, but her poor heart never recovered."

"I just wish I could get hold of those guys who wouldn't let the captain take his wife," said Peter angrily.

"Well, it was awfully sad," said Felicity, wiping her eyes. "But it was long ago, and we can't do any good by crying over it now. Let's go get something to eat. I made some nice little rhubarb tarts this morning."

We went. In spite of new disappointments and old heartbreaks, we still had appetites. And Felicity did make scrumptious rhubarb tarts!

# Magic Seed

<hr />

*"We should have known better than to trust Billy Robinson," said Felicity. "After all, what can you expect from a pig but a grunt?"*

## Chapter Two

We all had been working hard collecting money for the library fund. When we counted our money, we found that Peter had the largest amount—three dollars. Felicity was second with two dollars and fifty cents. The eggs she had been collecting to raise money sold well.

"If you had to pay Father for all the extra wheat you fed to the hens so they would lay well, you wouldn't have made so much, *Miss* Felicity," said Dan. We could tell he was jealous.

"I didn't feed them extra," Felicity said defensively. "Aunt Olivia's hens have been laying well too, and she fed them herself."

"Never mind," said Cecily. "We all have something to give except poor Sara Ray. I still can't believe her mother wouldn't let her collect for the library. What would it have hurt? I just don't understand her mother."

"I bet Sara Ray's really whining around today, feeling bad with nothing to give," Felix commented.

"Well, so would you," said Cecily.

"Hey look, here she comes up the hill now," said Peter. "And she isn't whining and crying; she's smiling."

When Sara Ray smiled (and she didn't waste her smiles on just any old thing or person), she almost seemed pretty. She had a couple of cute dimples, and her teeth were small and white, like little pearls. All her teeth were showing as she burst through the door into our kitchen.

"Look at this!" she cried excitedly, dumping a large amount of money onto our table. "I had a letter today from my Uncle Arthur in Winnipeg, and he sent me three dollars! He said I was to use it anyway I liked. Now Ma can't refuse to let me give it to the library. She thinks it's an awful waste, but she always goes by what Uncle Arthur says. The best part is that I prayed and prayed that some money might come, and now it has! See what praying does!"

We all knew that Sara Ray had been praying for some money to give, but none of us thought it would happen. I'm afraid we didn't rejoice as much as we should have, either. We had all earned our contributions by working hard or "begging." Somehow it didn't seem right that hers had just fallen out of the sky—as much a miracle as anything we had ever seen.

"She did pray for it you know," said Felix, after Sara Ray left for home. "I guess that's hard work, too."

"That's too easy a way of earning money," grumbled Peter. He was upset that now he and Sara Ray would have to share first place in the collecting contest we had set up between ourselves. "If the rest of us had just sat down and prayed, how much do you s'pose we'd have? It don't seem fair to me."

"Oh well, it's different with Sara," said Dan. "We *could* earn money and she *couldn't*. But let's go down to the orchard. The Story Girl got a letter from her father today, and she's going to read it to us."

We headed to the orchard quickly. A letter from the Story Girl's father was an event. To hear her read it was almost as good as hearing her tell a story.

Uncle Blair, who had just been a name to us before we came to Carlisle, was now very real. Our grown-ups didn't seem to approve of him very much. He belonged to a different world than theirs. Since the Story Girl's mother died, he hadn't been content at home. He'd taken to traveling the world, spending the fortune he had made as an artist; and occasionally doing some outstanding piece of art, for a good price. He adored the Story Girl. But not enough, it seemed, to arrange for her to be with him. That always seemed to cause the Story Girl to be sad. She missed him greatly and just lived for his letters and the occasional gifts he sent from around the world.

The Story Girl was said to look a lot like her father. People said her creative way of telling stories was inherited from him, but it was clear from his letters that Uncle Blair was a good writer, too.

Felix and I had always been a little ashamed of our father's letters to us from South America. Father could talk well, but as Felix said, he couldn't "write worth a cent." The letters we received from him were just scrawls telling us to be good boys and not to be any trouble for Uncle Alec and Aunt Janet. He always said he missed us, though, and was lonely without us. We were glad to get his letters, but we never read them to everybody in the circle in the orchard, as we did with Sara's letters from her father.

In this most recent letter, Uncle Blair said that he was spending the summer in Switzerland. He described the mountain lakes, crystal air, and snow-covered Alps. His letter included a tale of "The Prisoner of Chillon," written by a famous poet, Lord Byron. It was all so romantic. It made us want to travel and see the world.

"It must be splendid to go to Europe," sighed Cecily longingly.

"I'm going someday," said the Story Girl.

We looked at her with awe. In those days, Europe seemed as far away as the moon. It was hard to believe that one of us would ever go there.

But Aunt Julia had gone—and *she* had been brought up in Carlisle on the same farm. So it was possible that the Story Girl might go, too.

"What will you do there?" asked Peter practically.

"I'll learn how to tell stories to all the world," said the Story Girl dreamily.

It was a lovely golden-brown evening. The orchard and farmlands around us were full of kissing shadows. Over in the east, above the Awkward Man's house, floated the wispy clouds we called the Wedding Veil of the Proud Princess. We sat there looking at them and remembering the sad tale the Story Girl had told of the princess who was so proud. While we talked, the first star of the evening appeared.

All of a sudden, I remembered that I needed to take my dose of magic seed to help me grow. I was beginning to lose faith in the seeds, as they hadn't helped a bit as far as I could see. I ran into the house, took the box of seeds out of my trunk, and swallowed the pinch I was supposed to take. Just then, I heard Dan's voice behind me.

"Beverley King, what have you got there?"

I dropped the box quickly back into the trunk. "None of your business," I said defiantly.

"Yes it is." Dan was too much of a good friend to resent what I had said. "Look here, Bev, is that magic seed? And did you get it from Billy Robinson?"

I looked at Dan, suspicion growing in my mind.

"What do you know about Billy Robinson and his magic seed?" I demanded.

"Just this. I bought a box from him for . . . for something. He said he wasn't going to sell any of it to anybody else. Did he sell it to you?"

"Yes, he did," I said in disgust, beginning to understand that Billy's magic seed was a fraud.

"What for? *Your* mouth is a decent size," said Dan.

"Mouth? It had nothing to do with my mouth! He said it would make me grow tall. And it hasn't—not an inch! I don't see what you wanted it for! You are tall enough."

"I got it for my mouth," said Dan with a silly grin. "The girls in school laugh at my mouth. They say it looks like a big gash in a pie. Billy said that the magic seed would shrink it for sure."

Well! It seemed Billy had deceived us both—and not only us. We didn't find out the whole story until summer was over. Billy had deceived every student at Carlisle school in some way or another. We had all bought magic seed, promising to keep it a secret.

Felix had believed it would make him thin. Cecily was told her hair would become curly overnight, and Sara Ray was assured that she would no longer be afraid of old Peg Bowen. Felicity was supposed to become as clever as the Story Girl, and the Story Girl was told she would become a good cook like Felicity. We didn't find out for a long time what good the seed was supposed to do for Peter. But finally, he confessed to me that he had taken it to make Felicity like him. Billy had played on all of our weaknesses. He was nothing but a big deceiver. It made us feel even worse when we discovered that we had paid good money for plain old caraway seed that grew in Billy's backyard.

We didn't tell anyone about being hoaxed. If Uncle Roger had found out, he never would have stopped teasing us.

"We should have known better than to trust Billy Robinson," said Felicity. "After all, what can you expect from a pig but a grunt?"

We weren't surprised to learn that Billy Robinson was the winner of the library fund contest. He, of course, had the largest contribution—our money!

"I hope his conscience bothers him," said Cecily scornfully.

"Don't count on it," I said. "His conscience isn't anything like yours, Cece. He won't be bothered at all that he ripped us off." And he wasn't.

# The Magic Lantern Show

~~~❧~~~

*Sara would not give up the tempting delights
of the magic lantern show. So she walked on
in the way that sinners often do—miserable
and frightened. Even an eleven-year-old
sinner has a hard time when doing wrong.*

# Chapter Three

"I hate the thought of growing up," said the Story Girl. "I won't be able to go barefooted then, and nobody will ever see what beautiful feet I have."

She was sitting on the ledge of the open hay-loft window in Uncle Roger's barn. The July sun was shining down on her bare feet sticking out from beneath her print skirt. And they *were* beautiful. They were thin and shapely and satin smooth with dainty toes and nails like little pink shells.

We were all in the hay loft. The Story Girl had been telling us a story. Felicity and Cecily were all curled up in a corner, and we boys were lying idly on the sun-warmed hay. We had helped put the hay in the loft that morning for Uncle Roger, and we felt we had earned the right to laze around on our sweet-smelling couches.

Hay lofts are delicious places with just enough shadows and soft, uncertain noises to give the place an air of mystery. Sleek brown swallows flew in and out of their nests above our heads. Whenever a sunbeam shone through the slits in the logs of the barn, lovely golden dust shimmered in the air.

It was a perfect summer day outside with gobs of fluffy clouds floating above the spruce trees. Way off in the distance, we could see the blue gulf with little sailboats bobbing up and down. From where we sat, they looked like tiny white dots.

Pat, the Story Girl's cat, was prowling about, making frantic leaps trying to catch the swallows. We all felt content and in our right place that day. Until . . .

"I think it's vain to talk about your feet as being beautiful," commented Felicity. Her remark jarred our contentedness.

"I am not a bit vain," argued the Story Girl sincerely. "There's nothing wrong with knowing your good points. It's stupidity if you don't. It's only prideful when you get puffed up about them. I am not a bit pretty. And I know it. My only good points are my hair, eyes, and feet. So I think it's too bad that my feet have to be covered up all the time. I'm always glad when it gets warm enough to go barefooted. But when I grow up, they'll have to be covered all the time. It's just awful."

"You'll have to put your shoes and stockings on when you go to the magic lantern show tonight," said Felicity happily.

"Oh, I don't know. I'm thinking of going bare-footed," said the Story Girl in a mocking tone.

"Oh, you wouldn't! Sara Stanley, you're just kidding!" Felicity's blue eyes were filled with horror.

The Story Girl winked with her eye closest to Felix and me. But the side of her face that was next to Felicity's didn't move a muscle. She dearly loved to get a rise out of Felicity if she could.

"Why not? What's the difference between bare feet and bare hands and face? If they're clean, why not go barefooted?"

"Oh, but you wouldn't! It would be a disgrace!" said poor Felicity. She was really upset.

"We went to school barefooted all June," argued the Story Girl with a wicked little smile. "What's the difference between going barefooted to the schoolhouse in the daytime and going barefooted to the magic show in the evening?"

"Oh, there's a *lot* of difference. I just can't explain it, but everyone knows there *is* a difference. You know it yourself. Oh, please don't do such a thing, Sara."

"Well, I guess I won't since you seem to mind it so much," said the Story Girl. She really would have died a hundred deaths before she would have gone to a public meeting barefooted. But silly Felicity never seemed to catch on when she was being teased.

We were all rather excited over the magic lantern show, and we all were planning to go. Even Felix and I were excited, though we'd seen many such shows in Toronto. The traveling show had never been in Carlisle before.

Peter was excited, too. He went everywhere with us, including church and Sunday school. No one could point a finger at his behavior. He acted just like all of us. You never would have known he was a hired boy. The Story Girl took all the credit for getting him started going to church.

Felicity still had some problems when Peter stood up in church to sing. She declared you could always see the patch on his trousers, and it embarrassed her. But we paid no attention to Felicity and her prideful ways. Aunt Olivia kept Peter's stockings darned neatly, and she had also given him a Bible.

"I think I'll wrap it up and keep it in my box," he said. "I've an old Bible of Aunt Jane's at home I can use. I s'pose it's just the same, even if it is old, isn't it?"

"Oh yes," Cecily assured him. "The Bible is always the same."

"I thought maybe they'd got some new improvements on it since Aunt Jane's day," said Peter relieved.

"Here comes Sara Ray up the lane," announced Dan. He was looking out a knothole on the opposite side of the hay loft. "Looks like she's cryin'."

"What else is new?" remarked Felicity in a nasty tone. "She's always crying. She cries half the time. I'm sure she cries a full quart of tears each month."

"There are times when you can't help crying," said Cecily sympathetically, "but I hide it. Sara just goes ahead and cries, even in public."

When Sara Ray joined us, we soon knew *why* she was crying. Her mother wouldn't let her go to the magic lantern show that night. We all felt sorry for her.

"Yesterday your mother said you could go," said the Story Girl indignantly. "What made her change her mind?"

"She says there's measles in Markdale," sobbed Sara. "She says Markdale is full of 'em, and she's sure people from Markdale will be there. She won't let me go. I've never seen a magic lantern show—I've never seen *anything*."

"I don't believe there's any danger of catching measles," said Felicity. "If there was, we wouldn't be allowed to go either."

"I wish I *would* get the measles," Sara said defiantly. "Then maybe Ma would pay some attention to me."

"What if Cecily goes down with you and coaxes your mother?" suggested the Story Girl. "Perhaps she'd let you go then. She likes Cecily. She doesn't like

Felicity and me. It would only make things worse for us to try."

"Ma's gone to town. Pa and her went this afternoon, and they're not coming back 'til tomorrow. There's nobody home but Judy Pineau and me."

"Then," said the Story Girl, "why don't you just go to the show anyhow? Your mother won't ever know if you coax Judy not to tell."

"Oh, but that's wrong," said Felicity. "You shouldn't put Sara up to disobeying her mother."

Now for once Felicity was right. The Story Girl's suggestion *was* wrong. If it had been Cecily who protested, the Story Girl probably would have listened to her. But Felicity only drove the Story Girl on her sinful way. The rest of us kept our mouths shut. We knew a bad thing when we saw it. But the Story Girl was bound to tempt poor Sara Ray to disobey in spite of Felicity's warning.

"I have a good mind to do it," said Sara Ray. "But I can't get my good clothes. They're in the spare room and Ma locked the door. She put the fruitcake in there and locked it up, so we wouldn't eat it. So I don't have a thing to wear except my gingham school dress."

"Well, that's new and pretty," said the Story Girl. "We'll lend you some things. You can have my lace collar. It will look nice with your gingham dress. And I'm sure Cecily will lend you her second-best hat."

"But I've no shoes or stockings. They're locked up, too."

"You can borrow a pair of my shoes, and I've plenty of socks," said Felicity generously.

Sara decided to do it. When the Story Girl tempted us to do anything, we usually followed her. That evening when we started for the schoolhouse, Sara Ray was with us. She looked lovely in her borrowed clothes.

"Suppose she *does* catch the measles?" Felix whispered to us guys.

"Don't worry about it," said the Story Girl, overhearing. "The magic show will be in Markdale next week. All of the Markdale people will wait for it to go there."

The early evening was cool and dewy as we walked over the hills to the schoolhouse. The sky was creamy yellow with streaks of red. The moon hung low over the valley, and the air smelled sweet with the scent of newly-mown hay. Wild roses grew thickly along the fences, and the grass at the roadside was dusted with buttercups. Oh, how we loved the country!

I enjoyed our walk to the little whitewashed schoolhouse in the valley. But the others who had gone along with the Story Girl and tempted Sara Ray to disobey didn't seem to enjoy it much. Sara Ray herself was not happy. Her face was so sad that the Story Girl lost all patience with her. The Story Girl was not at ease either, though. I think her conscience was bothering her, but she wouldn't admit it.

"Now Sara," she said. "You just take my advice and go into this evening with all your heart. Never mind if it's bad. There's no use in being naughty if you spoil your fun by wishing all the time you were being good. You can repent afterward, but there is no use in mixing the two together."

"I'm not repenting," argued Sara. "I'm only scared of Ma finding out."

"Didn't Judy Pineau promise she wouldn't tell?"

"Yes, but maybe someone who sees me there will mention it to Ma."

"Well, if you're so scared, maybe you'd better not go. It isn't too late. There's your own house just ahead," said Cecily.

But Sara would not give up the tempting delights of the magic lantern show. So she walked on in the way that sinners often do—miserable and frightened. Even an eleven-year-old sinner has a hard time when doing wrong.

The magic show was lots of fun. The pictures were beautiful, and the man who was giving the presentation was funny and told lots of jokes. We repeated them on the way home, laughing again and again. Sara Ray, who didn't enjoy any part of the show, was a bit more cheerful on the way home. She seemed relieved that it was over. But the Story Girl didn't seem happy at all.

"Did you see the Markdale people?" she asked me quietly. "Those were the Williamsons who live next door to the Cowans. The Cowans have the measles at their house. I wish I'd never urged Sara to go against her mother's wishes. Don't tell Felicity I said so. If Sara Ray had enjoyed the show, I wouldn't mind. But I could tell she didn't. So I've done wrong and caused her to do wrong, and we have nothing to show for it."

Everyone but the Story Girl was trying to be cheerful as we walked along. The night was dark and starry, and we could see the Milky Way like a shimmering ribbon of stars in the heavens.

"There's four hundred million stars in the Milky Way," said Peter suddenly. We were astonished. He knew a whole lot more than a hired boy was expected to know. He had a sharp memory and never forgot anything he heard or read. He had nearly memorized the books his Aunt Jane had left him. Felix and I often felt he knew more than we did.

When he made the comment about the Milky Way, Felicity dropped behind to walk with him. His knowledge about the stars fascinated her. She hadn't wanted anything to do with him on the way to the show because he was barefooted. But now, after dark, no one would notice he had no shoes. I thought to myself that Felicity had more interest in Peter than even she realized.

We walked Sara Ray all the way to her door. She was afraid the old woman, Peg Bowen, would catch her if she went alone. Then the Story Girl and I walked up the lane together. Peter and Felicity lagged behind. Cecily and Dan and Felix were walking hand in hand in front of us, singing a hymn. Cecily had a very sweet voice, and I listened with delight. But the Story Girl sighed.

"What if Sara Ray does get the measles?" she asked miserably.

"Everyone has to have the measles sometime," I said, trying to comfort her. "And the younger you are the better."

# The Story Girl Does Penance

"I'm not going to do anything I like, and
I am going to do everything I can think
of that I don't like. It will be my way
of punishing myself for being so wicked,"
the Story Girl said.

# Chapter Four

Ten days later, Aunt Olivia and Uncle Roger stayed in town overnight. Peter and the Story Girl stayed with us at Uncle Alec's while they were gone.

Some of us were in the orchard at sunset listening to the Story Girl tell the story of "King Cophetua and the Beggar Maid." All of us were there except Peter, who was hoeing turnips, and Felicity, who had gone down the hill on an errand to Sara Ray's house.

The Story Girl was acting out the story and did it so well that we had no trouble believing the king would marry the beggar maid. I had read the story before and thought it was a bunch of rot. Surely no king would marry a beggar when he could have any princess he wanted. But then I understood it all.

Felicity came back with an anxious expression on her face. We could tell she had news. And she did.

"Sara is real sick," she said in a worried tone. "She has a cold, a sore throat, and a fever. Mrs. Ray says that if she isn't better by morning, she's going to send for the doctor. She's afraid it's the *measles*."

Felicity flung the last sentence like an accusation at the Story Girl, who turned pale.

"Oh, do you suppose she caught them at the magic lantern show?" she asked miserably.

"Where else would she catch them?" said Felicity mercilessly. "I didn't see her, of course. Mrs. Ray met me at the door and told me not to come in. She says the measles always go awful with the Ray family. If they don't die completely, it leaves them deaf or blind or something terrible like that." Seeing the misery in the Story Girl's eyes, Felicity added, "Of course, she may not have them at all."

But the Story Girl was not to be comforted. Felicity's words had done their work.

"I'd give anything if I'd never put Sara up to going to the show," she said. "It's all my fault, but the punishment falls on Sara, and that isn't fair. I'd go this minute and confess the whole thing to Mrs. Ray. But if I did, it might get Sara into more trouble. I won't sleep a wink tonight."

I don't think she did. She came down to break-fast the next morning looking very pale and sad.

"I'm going to do penance all day for coaxing Sara to disobey her mother," she announced.

"Penance?" we murmured. We had no idea what she was talking about.

"Yes. I'm not going to do anything I like, and I am going to do everything I can think of that I don't like. It will be my way of punishing myself for being so wicked. And if any of you think of anything that would punish me, just mention it. I thought it all out last night. Maybe Sara won't be so sick if God sees I'm truly sorry."

"He can see it anyhow, without your doing anything," said Cecily.

"Well, my conscience will feel better," she replied.

"I don't believe Presbyterians ever do—penance," said Felicity sounding doubtful. "I never heard of one doing it."

The rest of us thought it was probably a good thing for Sara Stanley to do penance, seeing that she was the one who had caused Sara Ray's problem. We felt sure she would do it . . . well, like she did everything else.

"You might put peas in your shoes," suggested Peter. "That would punish you for sure."

"That's a great idea, Peter," she responded. "I never thought of that. I'll get some after breakfast. I'm not going to eat a single thing all day, except bread and water—and not much of that!"

This was indeed heroic. Who could stand to sit down to one of Aunt Janet's meals and not eat? We felt *we* could never do it. But the Story Girl was going to try. We admired and pitied her.

Aunt Janet, of course, noticed the Story Girl wasn't eating and asked if she were sick.

"No. I am just doing penance, Aunt Janet, for a sin I committed. I can't confess it, because that would bring trouble on another person. So I'm going to punish myself all day. You don't mind, do you?"

Aunt Janet was in a very good humor that morning, so she just laughed. "Not if you don't go too far with your nonsense," she said.

"Thank you. And will you give me a handful of hard peas after breakfast, Aunt Janet? I want to put them in my shoes."

"There aren't any peas. I used the last of them in the soup yesterday."

"Oh," said the Story Girl, showing her disappointment. "Then I suppose I'll have to do without. The new peas wouldn't hurt enough. They're so soft they'd just squash flat."

"Tell you what," said Peter. "I'll pick up a lot of those little round stones on Mr. King's front walk. They'll be just as good as peas in your shoes."

"You'll do nothing of the sort," said Aunt Janet. "Sara must not do penance that way. She would wear holes in her stockings, and she might seriously bruise her feet."

"What would you say if I took a whip and whipped my bare shoulders till the blood came?" asked the Story Girl. She was determined to find something that would really hurt.

"I wouldn't *say* anything," retorted Aunt Janet. "I'd just turn you over my knee and give you a solid spanking, Miss Sara. You'd find that penance enough."

The Story Girl's face turned red with anger. To have such a remark made to a fourteen and a half year old—and in front of the boys, too. Really! Aunt Janet could sometimes be downright mean.

There wasn't much to do that day. We finally decided to go out in the orchard to play, but the Story Girl wouldn't come. She sat in the darkest, hottest corner of the kitchen with a piece of old cotton cloth in her hand.

"I'm not going out to play today," she said. "I'm not going to tell a single story. Aunt Janet won't let me put pebbles in my shoes. But I have put an old thistle burr next to the skin on my back. It sticks me if I lean back at all. And I'm going to make buttonholes all over this cotton piece. I *hate* making buttonholes more than anything in the world, so I'm going to make them all day."

"What good is making buttonholes on an old rag?" asked Felicity.

"It isn't any good at all. But the idea of penance is to make you feel uncomfortable. So it doesn't matter what you do, whether it's useful or not. Just as long as it's nasty.

"Oh, I wonder how Sara Ray is this morning?"

"Mother's going down this afternoon," said Felicity. "She says none of us can go near Sara's house 'til we know whether it's the measles or not."

"I've thought of a great penance for you," said Cecily eagerly. "Don't go to the missionary meeting tonight."

The Story Girl looked pitiful.

"I thought of that myself—but I *can't* stay home, Cecily. It would be more than I could stand. I *must* hear that missionary speak. They say he was almost eaten by cannibals once. Just think how many new stories I'll tell after I hear him. No, I have to go, but I tell you what I'll do. I'll wear my school dress and hat. *That* will be penance for sure. I hate that old dress. And Felicity, when you set the table tonight, put the knife with the broken handle at my place. I hate it so. And I'm drinking medicinal tea every two hours. That stuff is *awful*," she said, making a face. "It's supposed to be a good blood purifier though. Aunt Janet can't object to it."

The Story Girl was as good as her word. She sat right there in the hot kitchen and allowed herself no breaks. Sweat poured down her face, and she drank that horrible tea until she was almost sick. The cotton rag was filled with buttonholes galore.

But I did think Felicity was mean. She baked some little raisin cakes there in the kitchen and ate two of them right in front of the poor Story Girl. Felicity knew raisin cakes were Sara Stanley's favorite sweet, but she brought all the rest of them out to us in the orchard. Poor Sara could see us through the window. We were eating and having fun.

She just sat there making those horrible buttonholes. She wouldn't read the new magazine Dan brought from the post office or the letter that came from her father. Paddy, her cat, came over and purred his sweetest purrs, but she wouldn't even allow herself the pleasure of petting him.

Aunt Janet didn't get to go down the hill to Sara Ray's that afternoon, because company was coming to tea. It was the Millwards from over at Markdale. He was a doctor and Aunt Janet wanted everything to be as nice as possible. She sent us to our rooms to wash and dress up.

The Story Girl slipped over to her own house, and when she came back, we were all shocked. She had combed her hair out straight and had braided it in a tight, kinky braid. She wore an old faded print dress with holes in the elbows that was much too short for her. She looked terrible!

"Sara Stanley, are you crazy?" demanded Aunt Janet. "What do you mean by putting on such an outfit! Don't you know I'm having company for tea?"

"Yes, and that's why I put it on, Aunt Janet. I want to 'mortify the flesh,'" she said quoting the Scripture.

"I'll 'mortify' you if I catch you showing yourself to the Millwards like that, my girl! You go right home and dress yourself decently—or eat your supper in the kitchen."

The Story Girl chose to eat in the kitchen. She was terribly upset. I honestly think she would have loved to sit at the dining room table with company, looking her ugliest in that shabby, outgrown dress.

When we went to the missionary meeting that evening, the Story Girl wore her school dress and hat. And she had tied her hair up with the ugliest brown ribbon I'd ever seen. Felicity and Cecily had on their prettiest muslin dresses.

The first person we saw on the church porch was Mrs. Ray. She told us that Sara Ray didn't have the measles, only a bad cold. All of us were very glad and the Story Girl was radiant.

"Now you see, all your foolish penance was wasted," said Felicity as we walked home.

We were walking quite close together as old Peg Bowen's house was just ahead.

"Oh, I don't know," answered the Story Girl. "I feel better since I punished myself. It really was wrong of me to tempt Sara to disobey her mother, and I think I've learned better. But I'm going to make up for it tomorrow. In fact, as soon as I get home, I'm going straight to the pantry to see what I can find to eat."

"You won't find any raisin cakes," snapped Felicity in a nasty tone.

"I won't mind that. Anything at all will be better than medicinal tea. And I also have Father's letter to look forward to before I go to bed.

"Wasn't that missionary splendid? I'm trying to remember every word of that cannibal story he told. I want to tell it just like he did. Missionaries are such noble people."

"I'd like to be a missionary and have adventures like that," Felix said.

"I suppose," said Felicity in her all-knowing way. "I'm sure you'd be a fine piece of meat for those cannibals, Felix."

"It would be all right being a missionary if you could be sure the cannibals would be interrupted before they ate you like they were with that guy," said Dan.

"Nothing would prevent cannibals from eating Felix if they caught him," giggled Felicity. "He's so nice and fat."

I don't think my brother felt very much like a missionary when she said that. In fact, he looked like he was tempted to eat *her*.

"I'm going to put two cents more a week in my missionary box than I've been doing," said Cecily with determination.

Two cents more a week out of Cecily's egg money was quite a sacrifice for her. It inspired the rest of us. We all decided to increase what we gave weekly. And Peter, who had no missionary box at all, decided to start one.

"I don't seem to be able to feel as int'rested in missionaries as you guys do," he said. "But maybe if I begin to give somethin', I'll get in'trested. I'll want to know how my money's being spent. When your father's run away and your mother takes in washing, you can't give much to the heathens. But I'll do the best I can.

"My Aunt Jane liked missionaries a lot," he continued. "Are there any Methodist heathens? I s'pose I ought to give my box to them, rather than to the Presbyterian heathens."

"No, it's only after they're converted that they're anything in particular," said Felicity. "Before that they're just plain heathens. But if you want your money to go to a Methodist missionary, you can give it to the Methodist minister at the Markdale church. I guess the Presbyterians can look after their own heathens."

"Just smell Mrs. Sampson's flowers," said Cecily as we passed the Samson home. "Her roses are all out, and that bed of Sweet William is really beautiful."

"Sweet William is an awful name for a flower," said the Story Girl. "William is a man's name, and men are *never* sweet. They are many nice things, but they are *not* sweet and shouldn't be. Sweet is for women.

"Oh, look at how the moon is shining on the road," the Story Girl continued. "I'd like a dress of moonlight with stars for buttons."

"It wouldn't do," said the practical Felicity, who didn't have an ounce of imagination in her. "You could see right through it."

That seemed to settle the question of dresses made of moonlight.

# Rachel Ward's Blue Chest

"Who on earth was Cousin Rachel Ward?
And why were her wedding things shut up in
an old blue chest in Uncle Alec's kitchen? We
demanded the story at once, and the Story
Girl told it as she peeled her potatoes."

# Chapter Five

It was a hot day in August, and the grown-ups were all in a dither about something. We hung around the kitchen, snitching things to eat and trying to listen to their discussion.

"It's utterly out of the question," said Aunt Janet seriously. When Aunt Janet said anything *seriously*, it just meant that she was seriously thinking about it and would probably do it. They were talking about the wedding of Uncle Edward's daughter. He had written asking all the aunts and uncles to come over to Halifax, Nova Scotia, for the wedding and stay for a week. Uncle Alec and Aunt Olivia were eager to go, but Aunt Janet thought it was impossible.

"How could we go away and leave the farm with all of these young ones?" she demanded. "We'd come home and find them all sick and the house burned down."

"Not necessarily," said Uncle Roger. "Felicity is as good a housekeeper as you are. I'll stay here and look after them all, so they won't burn the house down. You've been promising Edward for years to visit him, and you'll never have a better chance. The haying is over and the harvest isn't on yet. Alec needs a change. He isn't looking well at all."

I think it was Uncle Roger's last argument that convinced Aunt Janet. In the end, she decided to go. Uncle Roger's house was to be locked up, and he and Peter and the Story Girl were to stay with us.

We were all delighted. Felicity was especially happy to be left in charge. She was in seventh heaven to have three meals a day to prepare, cows and chickens and the garden to look after, and all of us to boss. Of course, we were supposed to help, but she was to "run things." She couldn't wait.

The Story Girl was pleased, too. "Felicity is going to give me cooking lessons," she confided as we walked in the orchard. "Isn't that great? I ought to be able to learn something in a week, don't you think? It will be easier when there are no grown-ups around to make me nervous when I make mistakes."

Uncle Alec and the aunts left on Monday morning. Poor Aunt Janet was full of fear and gave us so many warnings that we couldn't remember any of them. Uncle Alec merely told us to be good and mind Uncle Roger. Aunt Olivia laughed at us, flashing her pansy-blue eyes and said she knew we'd have a fun vacation without all of them.

"Be sure they go to bed on time," Aunt Janet called back to Uncle Roger as they drove out of the gate. "And if anything terrible happens, telegraph us." Then they were really gone, and we were left to "keep house."

Uncle Roger and Peter went to work out in the field, and Felicity started to get things together to prepare supper. She gave each of us our jobs. The Story Girl was to peel the potatoes. Dan and I were to pick the peas from the garden and shell them. Cecily was to build and take care of the fire in the old woodstove. I was to peel the turnips. Then Felicity made our mouths water by announcing that she was going to make a roly-poly jam pudding for dessert.

I peeled my turnips on the back porch and put them in a pot of water all ready to boil. My job took less time than some of the others' jobs, so I had time to watch them. The kitchen was a beehive of activity. The Story Girl peeled her potatoes—a little slowly and awkwardly. She really wasn't much good in the kitchen. Dan and Felix shelled the peas. But, of course, they had to fool around a bit by attaching some of the peapods to Paddy's ears and tail. Poor old Pat ran around the yard trying to shake them off while we boys howled at his antics. Felicity, all flushed and serious, measured and stirred like an old housewife.

"I am sitting on a tragedy," said the Story Girl suddenly.

Felix and I stared. We were not quite sure what a "tragedy" was, but we sure didn't think it was the blue wooden chest on which she sat.

The chest filled up the corner between the table and the wall. We had hardly noticed it before. It was very large and heavy, and Felicity always complained about the "old thing" when she had to sweep around it.

"This chest holds a tragedy," explained the Story Girl. "I know a story about it."

"Cousin Rachel Ward's wedding things are all in that old chest," said Felicity.

Who on earth was Cousin Rachel Ward? And why were her wedding things shut up in a chest in Uncle Alec's kitchen? We demanded the story at once, and the Story Girl told it as she peeled her potatoes. Felicity said later that she should have paid more attention to her potatoes as a lot of them still had their black "eyes." We didn't care about the potatoes, but we did care about the story.

"It is a sad story," said the Story Girl. "It happened fifty years ago when Grandfather and Grandmother King were young. Grandmother's cousin, Rachel Ward, came to spend a winter with them. She was an orphan from Montreal. I have never heard what she looked like, but I think she must have been beautiful."

"Mother says she was awfully romantic and sentimental," interrupted Felicity.

"Well, anyway, she met Will Montague that winter. He was handsome. Everybody said so."

"And an awful flirt," said Felicity.

"Felicity, I *wish* you wouldn't interrupt," the Story Girl said. "It spoils the effect. What would you feel like if I kept stirring things into your pudding that didn't belong there? I feel just the same way when you interrupt my story.

"Well, anyway, Will Montague fell in love with Rachel Ward—and she with him. It was all arranged for them to be married here in the spring. Poor Rachel was so happy that winter. She made all of her wedding things with her own hands. That's what girls did back then, you know, for there was no such thing as a sewing machine. Well, in April, the wedding day came at last and all the guests were here. Rachel was dressed in her beautiful wedding gown and waiting for her bridegroom to come. And . . . ," the Story Girl laid down her knife and potato and clasped her hands dramatically, "Will Montague never came!"

We felt as much of a shock as if we had been one of the wedding guests.

"What happened to him? Did he get killed?" Cecily asked

The Story Girl sighed and returned to peeling her potatoes.

"No indeed! I wish he had been. *That* would have been suitable and romantic. No, it was horrid. He ran away because he was in debt. It was just terrible. He never sent a word to Rachel, and she never heard from him again."

"Pig!" said Felix.

"Rachel was brokenhearted, of course. When she found out what had happened, she took all of her wedding things, her supply of linens, and the presents that had been given to her and locked them in this old chest. Then she went back to Montreal and took the key with her. She never came back to the island again. I suppose she couldn't bear to. She has lived in Montreal ever since, an old maid, nearly seventy years of age. This chest has not been opened since she left."

"Mother wrote to Cousin Rachel ten years ago," said Cecily, "and asked her if she could open the chest to see if the moths had gotten into it. Cousin Rachel wrote back and said there was one thing in the trunk she didn't want anyone to see. Mother decided to leave it unopened. Ma said she wished she could get rid of it. It's so hard to move when the floor has to be scrubbed."

"What didn't she want anyone to see?" asked Felix.

"Ma thinks it was her wedding gown. But father says he believes it was Will Montague's picture," said Felicity. "He saw her put it in. Father knows some of the things that are in the chest. He was ten years old at the time, and he saw her pack it. There's a white muslin wedding gown and a veil . . . and . . . a . . . a . . . ," Felicity dropped her eyes and blushed.

"A petticoat, embroidered by hand from hem to belt," said the Story Girl calmly.

"And a china fruit basket with an apple on the handle," went on Felicity, relieved she didn't have to say "petticoat" in front of the boys. "And a tea set and a blue candlestick."

"I'd love to see all the things that are in it," said the Story Girl.

"Ma says it must never be opened without Cousin Rachel's permission," said Cecily.

Felix and I looked at the chest reverently. Now it had new importance in our eyes. It seemed like a tomb where a romance was buried.

"What happened to Will Montague?" I asked.

"Nothing!" said the Story Girl viciously. "He just went on, got out of debt, and came back here to the island. Now he's married to a nice girl who has money, and he's very happy. Just like a man!" she snapped.

"Beverley King," cried Felicity suddenly, peering into the turnip pot. "You've gone and put the turnips on to boil whole, just like potatoes."

Uncle Roger roared when he heard it. He also roared when he heard about Felix trying to milk the cow that morning. Apparently Felix and the cow didn't get along very well. She tramped on his foot and upset the bucket.

"What are you supposed to do when a cow won't stand straight?" spluttered Felix angrily.

"Now that's a good question, Felix," said Uncle Roger gravely.

Uncle Roger's laughter was one thing, but when he got serious, that was even harder to take.

In the pantry after dinner, the Story Girl, all wrapped up in an apron, was learning how to make bread. She had flour from head to toe. Under Felicity's watchful eyes, she had set the bread to rise and would bake it the next day.

"The first thing you must do tomorrow morning is knead the bread well," said Felicity as sternly as a mother would. "It's going to be a very warm night, so the sooner you do it in the morning, the better it will be." Felicity's superior tone made my blood boil. She might be a good cook, but she herself was hard to take. I thought it was going to be a long week with her in charge.

With that, we went to bed and slept soundly, dreaming of blue chests, crooked cows, and poorly cooked turnips.

# The Missing Baby

*"There was no doubt—Jimmy was gone.
We tore about the house and yard like
maniacs. We looked into every nook
and cranny—no Jimmy."*

# Chapter Six

It was five thirty the next morning when Felicity got us up. We were all yawning and grumbling at the early hour.

"Oh, dear me, I've overslept," Felicity said as we met on the steps. "I planned on getting up much earlier, because Uncle Roger likes to eat breakfast early. Well, I suppose the fire is going anyhow. The Story Girl is up. I guess she got up early to knead the bread dough. She couldn't sleep all night for worrying about it."

The fire was going and a flushed and happy Story Girl was taking a loaf of bread from the oven.

"Just look," she said proudly. "I have all the bread baked. I got up at three and it was lovely and light. I just gave it a good kneading and popped it into the oven. It's all done and ready to eat. But the loaves don't seem quite as large as they should be," she added doubtfully.

"Sara Stanley!" Felicity flew across the kitchen. "Do you mean that you put the bread dough right into the oven after you kneaded it, without leaving it to rise a second time?"

The Story Girl turned quite pale.

"Yes, I did," she faltered. "Wasn't that right, Felicity?"

"You've just ruined the bread," Felicity said flatly. "It's as heavy as a stone. Don't you have any sense at all? I'd rather have a little common sense than be a great storyteller."

"Please don't tell Uncle Roger," said the Story Girl, very close to tears.

"Oh, I won't tell him," promised Felicity. "He'll be sure to find out though. We'll have to eat old bread today. This will go to the chickens. It's an awful waste of good flour."

The Story Girl went out with Felix and me to the orchard while Dan and Peter went to work.

"It isn't any use for me to try to learn to cook," she said.

"Never mind," I said sympathetically. "You tell great stories."

"But what good would that do a hungry boy?" wailed the Story Girl.

"Boys ain't *always* hungry," responded Felix. "There's times when they ain't."

"I don't believe it," said the Story Girl in a depressed tone.

"Besides, you may learn to cook yet, if you keep trying."

"But Aunt Olivia would never allow waste. My only hope was to learn to cook this week. Now I suppose Felicity is so disgusted with me that she won't give me any more lessons."

"I don't care," said Felix. "I like you better than Felicity, even if you can't cook. Lots of folks can make bread. But there aren't many who can tell a story like you."

"But it's better to be useful than just interesting," sighed the Story Girl bitterly.

Felicity, who was useful, would have given anything to be interesting.

That afternoon company came. First came Aunt Janet's sister, Mrs. Patterson, with her daughter who was sixteen and her little two-year-old boy. They were followed by a buggy-load of Markdale people and finally, Mrs. Elder Frewen and her sister from Vancouver. The sister had two little girls with her.

"When it rains it pours," grumbled Uncle Roger as he went out to tie up their horses. Felicity was having a heyday. She had been baking all afternoon, even though she didn't know they were coming. She couldn't have been more pleased that she had wonderful goodies to show off. She didn't care if all of Carlisle came to tea.

Cecily set the table, and the Story Girl waited on everyone and washed the dishes. Felicity, of course, took all the credit and treated the other girls as though they were servants. She presided over the tea table like a queen. She seemed to know by instinct who took sugar and who wanted lemon. And she was so pretty, I could hardly eat for looking at her, even though I disliked her so much.

The Story Girl moped around, totally miserable after her bread mess. No one took any notice of her, and she didn't offer to tell a single story. It was Felicity's day for sure. After tea, Mrs. Frewen and her sister wanted to visit their father's grave in the Carlisle churchyard. Everybody wanted to go along for the walk. But someone had to stay with baby Jimmy Patterson, who had just fallen asleep on the sofa.

Dan volunteered to baby-sit. He said he had a new book to read and he'd just as soon stay behind and watch the baby.

"I think we'll be back before he wakes up," said Mrs. Patterson. "He's very good and won't be any trouble anyhow. Just don't let him go outside since he has a cold."

We went away leaving Dan sitting in the door-way reading and the baby sound asleep on the couch. Felix and the girls and I returned in about an hour to find Dan sitting in the same spot, and the baby was nowhere to be seen.

"Dan, where's the baby?" cried Felicity in alarm.

Dan looked around, his jaw falling open in amazement. I never saw anyone look so foolish.

"I don't know," he said helplessly.

"You've been all caught up in that book and don't know where he is," accused Felicity.

"I haven't," said Dan. "He *must* be in the house. I've been sitting right across the door ever since you left. He couldn't have gotten out unless he crawled right over me. He's got to be in the house."

"He isn't in the kitchen," said Felicity rushing about wildly. "We've got to find him before his mother comes. He couldn't have gotten into the other part of the house, for I shut the hall door tight. No baby could open it—and it's still shut tight. So are all the windows. He *must* have gone out the door, Dan King, and it's your fault."

"He *didn't* go out this door," argued Dan stubbornly. "I know that."

"Well, where is he then?" she yelled. "Did he melt into air?" demanded Felicity. "Don't stand around like ninnies. All of you come and look. We have to find him before his mother comes. Dan King, you are an idiot!"

Dan was too frightened to resent what she had said to him. There was no doubt—Jimmy was gone. We tore about the house and yard like maniacs. We looked into every nook and cranny—no Jimmy.

Mrs. Patterson came, and we still had not found him. Things were getting serious. We got Uncle Roger and Peter from the field to help us look. Mrs. Patterson became hysterical. The ladies finally persuaded her to lie down in the spare room with some kind of a calming sedative.

Everybody was blaming poor Dan. Cecily asked him what he would feel like if we *never* found Jimmy. The Story Girl remembered some gruesome story about a baby in Markdale who had wandered away.

"They never found him 'til spring," she whispered. "Nothing was left but a *skeleton*—with grass growing through it."

"This beats me," said Uncle Roger after we had been looking for over an hour. "I do hope he hasn't wandered down to the swamp. It seems impossible that he could walk so far, but I must go and see. Felicity, hand me my high boots from under the sofa."

Felicity, pale and tearful, dropped to her knees and lifted the frill of the sofa.

"Oh look!" she uttered in an awed whisper. There, with his head pillowed on Uncle Roger's boots was Jimmy Patterson—still sound asleep.

"Well—I'll be jiggered!" said a relieved Uncle Roger.

"I *knew* he didn't go out the door," said Dan triumphantly.

When the last buggy had driven away, Felicity set some bread to rise. The rest of us sat around the back-porch steps in the twilight, eating cherries and throwing the pits at each other. Cecily had a question.

"What does it mean when you say, 'When it rains, it pours'?"

"Oh, it means if anything happens, something else is sure to happen," said the Story Girl. "For example: There's Mrs. Murphy. She never had a proposal in her life till she was forty. And then she had three in one week. She was so flustered that she took the wrong one and has been sorry ever since. Do you see what it means now?"

"I guess so," said Cecily doubtfully. Later on we heard her telling Felicity about her new knowledge. "'When it rains, it pours' means that nobody wants to marry you for ever so long, and then lots of people do."

# Forbidden Fruit

～～～

*"They taste great," Dan said, smacking his lips and letting the red juice run down his chin. He paid no attention to the horror on our faces or to Felicity's pleadings.*

# *Chapter Seven*

**A**ll of us in the King household were grumpy the next day. Only Uncle Roger was his usual happy self. I think we were all still upset over the disappearance of little Jimmy. Even though he had been found, we had all suffered a great scare. And we were also out of sorts about the snacks we had been eating before bed.

Felicity being "in charge" might have been a pain and a bore, but she *did* like sweets. She always looked the other way when we swiped stuff from the pantry before bed. I saw my brother, Felix, with three huge pieces of chocolate cake. That probably didn't help his waistline get any slimmer, and none of us slept well with our tummies stuffed full. Too much of the good life, I guess. Anyway, we were grumpy, and we had all been having bad dreams.

Dan had a grudge against his sister and made it plain to all of us at breakfast. He remembered Felicity's hard words to him when Jimmy Patterson was lost. And he was determined that Felicity wasn't going to boss him anymore.

It was not a pleasant day, and to make matters worse, it rained until mid-afternoon. The Story Girl was sulky. She had not forgotten her failure with bread-making the day before. Instead of sitting at the breakfast table with the rest of us, she sat on Rachel Ward's blue chest, picking away at her egg like a martyr. After breakfast, she washed the dishes and cleaned up her bedroom without saying a word to anyone. Then she disappeared with a book under one arm and Paddy, her cat, under the other. We knew she was escaping to the window seat in the upstairs hall, and no one would be able to coax her away from her reading.

Even Cecily, normally sweet and mild-mannered, was snappish and complained of a headache. Peter had gone home to see his mother, and Uncle Roger had gone to Markdale on business. Sara Ray came up to play but went home crying after Felicity snubbed her. Felicity began dinner preparations early, banging pots and pans around so much that Cecily begged her to be quiet.

Dan sat on the floor, whittling and making a mess to annoy Felicity. He succeeded perfectly.

"I wish Aunt Janet and Uncle Alec were home," said Felix. "It's not half as much fun having the grown-ups away as I thought it would be."

"I wish I were back in Toronto," I complained.

"I'm sure I wish you were, too," snapped Felicity.

"Anyone who lives with you, Felicity King, will always be wishing he was somewhere else!" said Dan.

"I wasn't talking to you, Dan King," retorted Felicity. "'Speak when you're spoken to; come when you're called,'" she quoted, mimicking her mother.

"Oh, I *wish* it would stop raining," wailed Cecily, who was now lying on the couch nursing her headache. "I *wish* my head would stop aching. I *wish* Ma had never gone away. I *wish* you'd leave Felicity alone, Dan."

"*I* wish girls had some sense," responded Dan, which brought the wishing to an end. The wishing fairy would have had the time of her life in the King kitchen that morning.

By tea time, things had brightened up. The rain had stopped, and the old kitchen with its low rafters was full of sunshine that danced on the floor and flickered over the table.

The Story Girl had taken a nap and seemed to have her good humor back. Cecily's headache had eased up, and all seemed right again—except for Dan. He was determined to be nasty, especially to his sister Felicity. He would not even laugh when the Story Girl began a funny story about their old minister, the reverend Mr. Scott.

She told it anyway. "When he got very old," she began, "the Presbyterian leaders thought it was time

for him to retire. He didn't think so, but they gently pressured him until he did. When he finally retired, a young minister was called to the Carlisle church. Mr. Scott moved away, but he often visited the church members.

"The new minister dreaded meeting the old minister, because he had heard Mr. Scott was upset at being set aside. One day the young minister was visiting the Crawfords when old Mr. Scott knocked at the back door. The young minister turned quite pale. Fearing an unpleasant confrontation, he begged Mrs. Crawford to hide him. She did. She hid him in the china closet just as Mr. Scott came in. He talked kindly, read the Bible to the Crawfords, and then began to pray. In those days, they prayed really long prayers. He prayed so long that the young minister in the closet was about to faint from lack of air. At the end of the prayer, the old minister said, 'Oh, Lord, bless the poor young minister hiding in the closet. Give him courage to face me. Make him a burning light to the congregation and use him greatly.'

"Can you imagine how the young minister felt?" asked the Story Girl. "He came out red-faced and gasping for air. They shook hands and from then on were the best of friends."

"How did the old minister know he was in the closet?" asked Felix.

"He never said, but they supposed maybe he had seen him through the window before he came into the house. If that's true, he could have spared the young man some torture by not talking and praying so long. I think old Mr. Scott may have thought it was a good joke, but the poor man nearly died from lack of air. I guess even ministers have mean streaks sometimes."

After supper that evening, once the milking chores were done, we all gathered in the orchard. We ate apples like greedy little pigs, and the Story Girl told us a tale about the Irishman's pig. It seemed that the pig made himself sick by eating "bad berries." Even when he was near death, he kept eating the berries that were poisoning him. We demanded to see the berries, and the Story Girl led us over to the thicket where they were growing. I don't know what kind of berries those red clusters were, but the Story Girl told us that we were forbidden to eat them. Just the same, Dan picked a bunch and held them up.

"Dan King, don't you dare eat those berries," said Felicity in her bossiest tone. "They're poisonous. Drop them right now!"

Now Dan had not even thought of eating them until his sister dared him. He would show her!

"I'll eat them if I please, Felicity King," he said in a fury. "I don't believe they're poisonous. See here!"

And with that he crammed the whole bunch into his big mouth and chewed them up.

"They taste great," he said, smacking his lips and letting the red juice run down his chin. He paid no attention to the horror on our faces or to Felicity's pleadings.

We feared he would drop dead before our eyes. But when an hour passed and nothing happened, we thought he was probably right after all. We admired him for being so daring and thought him to be quite a hero.

"I knew they wouldn't hurt me," he boasted. "Felicity's such a worrywart!"

When it started to get dark, we headed back to the house. I noticed that Dan was rather pale and quiet. He lay down on the sofa when we got back.

"Are you feeling bad, Dan?" I whispered anxiously.

"Shut up," he said.

I shut up.

Felicity and Cecily were getting our bedtime snacks together when we were startled by a loud groan from the sofa.

"Oh, I'm sick. I'm awful sick," said Dan. All the defiance and bravado had gone out of him. We all went to pieces, except Cecily. She was the only one who stayed cool in the crisis.

"Have you got a pain in your stomach?" she demanded.

"I've got an awful pain here, if that's where my stomach is. Oh . . . oh . . . oh," he moaned rolling around in pain.

"Go for Uncle Roger," commanded Cecily. She was pale but composed. "Felicity, put on the kettle. Dan, I'm going to give you mustard and warm water." Dan made a face. He took the awful stuff, but it gave him no relief. He continued to roll around and groan. It was awful to see. All of us were getting really frightened. When Uncle Roger came in the house, he sent Peter at once to get the doctor. Uncle Roger went down the hill to get Mrs. Ray who was well known for her nursing. Sara came too, but she might as well have stayed home. She did nothing but wring her hands and walk about asking if Dan was going to die.

Cecily was the one who calmed the storm in all of us. Felicity might have been able to charm us all with her cooking and the Story Girl with her stories, but Cecily was great in a crisis. She was like a ministering angel. She got Dan into bed and made him swallow every cure she could think of. She applied hot cloths to his abdomen until her hands were half burned off.

There was little doubt that Dan was suffering terribly. He kept groaning and crying for his mother.

"Oh, isn't it terrible!" said Felicity, wringing her hands as she walked the kitchen floor. "Oh, why doesn't the doctor come? I *told* Dan the berries were bad. But surely they can't *kill* people outright!"

"Many years ago, Pa's cousin got awful sick from eating something and died," sobbed Sara Ray.

"Hold your tongue," I said in a fierce whisper. "You oughta have more sense than to say such things to the other girls. They don't want to be any worse scared than they are."

"But Pa's cousin *did* die," she insisted.

"My Aunt Jane used to rub whiskey on for pain," suggested Peter.

"We haven't any whiskey," said Felicity with disapproval. "We don't allow any liquor in this house."

"But rubbing whiskey on the *outside* doesn't do no harm," argued Peter. "It's only when you take it inside that it's bad for you."

"Well, we don't have any anyhow," said Felicity. "Do you suppose blueberry wine would do?"

Peter didn't think blueberry wine would help.

It was ten o'clock before Dan began to get better. When the doctor finally came, he found his patient very weak and white but free from pain.

Dr. Grier patted Cecily on the head and told her she had done just the right thing. He examined some of the berries and said they were definitely poisonous.

He advised Dan not to touch any forbidden fruit in the future. Mrs. Ray decided to stay all night with us in case the crisis wasn't over.

"I'll be very glad for you to stay," said Uncle Roger. "I admit I feel a bit shook. I urged Janet and Alec to go to Halifax and took the responsibility of the children. I don't think I really knew what I was getting myself into. If anything had happened, I would never have forgiven myself."

As we went up the stairs, Felicity said drearily, "It's been a horrible day."

"I guess we made it horrible ourselves," said the Story Girl.

"I'll be glad for tomorrow to come," said Felicity. "Do you remember what Anne Shirley from over at Green Gables said? 'Tomorrow is another day with no mistakes in it.'"

"That will be great," responded the Story Girl.

We all felt that way.

# The Devil Made Him Do It

"'The Lord had nothing to do with it,'
said old Mr. Scott. 'It was the
McCloskeys and the devil.'"

## Chapter Eight

**D**an was better in the morning, although weak and pale. He wanted to get up, but Cecily ordered him to stay in bed. We were glad Felicity didn't tell him to, for he would never have obeyed. But Cecily wasn't so bossy and Dan agreed. Cecily carried his meals to him and read him one of his favorite books in her spare time.

The Story Girl went up and told him some fun stories and Sara Ray brought him a pudding she had made herself. Her intentions were good, but the pudding . . . well, he fed most of it to Paddy. The cat had curled up on the foot of Dan's bed and was encouraging the patient by purring loudly.

"Ain't Paddy just a great old fellow?" said Dan. "He knows I'm still not feeling good. He never pays attention to me when I'm well. I like having him here."

Felix and Peter and I were helping Uncle Roger do some work, and Felicity was indulging in house-cleaning—her favorite task. It was evening before we all got together in the orchard. In August, it was a place of shady sweetness, fragrant with the smell of ripening apples. Dusky shadows rimmed the distant hills with the sunset's backdrop. There was no such thing as hurrying in the world, while we lingered there, talking of anything that came into our minds.

The Story Girl told us a story about a prince and a princess and that led us to a discussion about kings. *What would it be like?* we wondered. Peter thought it would be fine but inconvenient to have to wear a crown all the time.

"Oh, but they don't," said the Story Girl. "Maybe they did once, but now they wear hats. Their crowns are just for special occasions. These days, they look like ordinary people."

"I'd like to see a queen though," said Cecily wishfully.

"The prince of Wales was in Charlottetown once," said Peter. "My Aunt Jane saw him up close."

"That was before we were born, and it won't likely happen again," said Cecily sadly.

"I think there were a lot more kings and queens long ago," said the Story Girl. "They seem awful scarce now. There isn't one in this country anywhere. Perhaps I'll get to see one when I go to Europe."

What she didn't know was that one day she would stand before a king and be honored. None of us knew that as we sat in the old orchard that night.

"Can a queen do exactly as she pleases?" asked Sara Ray.

"Not anymore," explained the Story Girl.

"A king can't do as he pleases either," said Felix. "If he tries to and it isn't what the people want, parliament or something squelches him."

"Isn't 'squelch' a lovely word?" commented the Story Girl. "It sounds just like what it does. It's so expressive. *Squ-u-elch*!"

It *was* a lovely word the way the Story Girl said it. "Uncle Roger says that Martin Forbes' wife has squelched *him*," said Felicity. "He says Martin can't call his soul his own since he got married."

"I'm glad of it," said Cecily forcefully.

We all stared. This was so unlike our mild-mannered Cecily.

"Martin Forbes is a horrid man who lives in Summerside. He called me Johnny!" she explained. "He was visiting here with his wife two years ago, and he called me Johnny every time he spoke to me. Can you imagine! I'll never forgive him."

"That isn't a Christian spirit," rebuked Felicity.

"I know a story about Martin Forbes' grandfather," said the Story Girl. "Long ago they didn't have a choir in the Carlisle church. At last, they got one, and Andrew McPherson was to sing bass in it. Old Mr. Forbes hadn't gone to church for years because of his rheumatism. But he went the first Sunday the choir sang, because he had never heard anyone sing bass. Grandfather King asked Mr. Forbes what he thought of the choir. Mr. Forbes answered in a strong Scottish accent, 'verra guid' (very good), but as for Andrew's bass, there was nae bass aboot it (no bass about it). It was just a *bur-r-r-r* the hale time' (whole time).'"

We rolled in the grass, howling with laugher at the way the Story Girl pronounced the words and did the "*bu-r-r-r-r.*"

"Poor Dan," said Cecily. "He's up there alone in his room, missing all the fun. I suppose it's mean of us to be having such a good time here when he has to stay in bed."

"If Dan hadn't done wrong by eating the bad berries when he was told not to, he wouldn't be sick," said Felicity, with no mercy. "You're bound to find trouble when you do wrong. It was thanks to the Lord that he didn't die."

"That makes me think of another story about old Mr. Scott," said the Story Girl. "You know, I told you he was very angry because the Presbyterian leaders made him retire. There were two ministers he blamed for it. One time a friend of his was trying to console him and said, 'You should be resigned to the will of the Lord.'

"'The Lord had nothing to do with it,' said old Mr. Scott. 'It was the McCloskeys and the devil.'"

"You shouldn't speak of the . . . the . . . *devil*," said Felicity, rather shocked.

"Well, that's just what Mr. Scott said."

"Oh, it's all right for a *minister* to speak of him. But it isn't nice for little girls. If you have to speak of . . . of . . . him, you might say Old Scratch. That is what mother calls him."

"Hmmm. I don't think that would do," decided the Story Girl.

"I don't think it hurts to mention the . . . the . . . that person when you're telling a story," said Cecily. "It's only in plain talking that it won't do. It sounds too much like swearing."

"I know another story about Mr. Scott," said the Story Girl. "Not long after he was married, his wife wasn't quite ready for church one morning when it was time to go. So, just to teach her a lesson, he drove off alone and left her to walk all the way. It was nearly two miles in the heat and dust.

"She took it very quietly. It's the best way I guess when you're married to a man like old Mr. Scott. But a few Sundays after that, he was late himself. I suppose she wanted to get even with him, for she slipped out of the house and drove off alone. Mr. Scott finally arrived at church all hot and dusty and in a bad temper. He went straight to the pulpit, leaned over it, and looked her square in the eye as she sat calmly in her pew. In his best Scotch accent, he said, 'It was clever of you, but don't try it again!'"

While we were laughing, Pat came down the walk waving his tale. Behind him came Dan, all dressed and ready to join in the fun.

"Do you think you should be up, Dan?" said Cecily anxiously.

"I had to," said Dan. "The window was open, and it was more than I could stand to hear all of you laughing and me missing it all. Besides, I'm all right again. I feel fine."

"I guess this will be a lesson to you, Dan King," Felicity said in her superior tone. "I guess you won't forget it in a hurry. You won't go eating the bad berries another time when you're told not to."

Dan had picked out a soft spot in the grass for himself and was just in the act of sitting down when she said it. I gasped as he stopped halfway down, straightened up, and turned an angry face to his sister. He was red as fire and didn't say a word as he stalked away.

"Now he's gone off mad," said Cecily in fear. "Oh Felicity, why couldn't you have held your tongue?"

"Why, what did I say to make him mad?" said the provoking girl.

"I think it's awful for brothers and sisters to be always quarreling," sighed Cecily. "The Cowans fight all the time. You and Dan will soon be as bad."

"Don't talk nonsense. Dan's gotten so touchy that it isn't safe to speak to him," spat Felicity. "I should think he'd be sorry for all the trouble he made last night. But you just take up for him in everything, Cecily."

"I don't!"

"You do! And you've no business doing it, especially since mother's away. She left *me* in charge."

"You didn't take much charge last night when Dan got sick," said Felix nastily. Felicity had told Felix that night at tea that he was getting fatter than ever. This was his way of getting back at her. "You were pretty glad to leave it all to Cecily then," he continued.

"Who's talking to you?" snapped Felicity.

"Now stop it, you two!" said the Story Girl. "Before you know it, we'll all be quarreling, and then we'll lose another day sulking around. It's stupid to spoil a whole day. Let's just all sit still and count to one hundred before anyone says another word."

We sat still and began counting. When Cecily finished she got up and went in search of Dan, hoping to soothe his feelings. Felicity called after her to tell her to tell Dan that she had saved a jam turnover for him. Felix held out a beautiful red apple to Felicity as a peace offering, and the Story Girl began another story. But we never heard it. Just then Cecily came flying through the orchard, wringing her hands.

"Oh, come, come quick!" she gasped. "Dan's eating the bad berries again—he's already eaten a whole bunch of them. He says he'll show Felicity. I can't stop him. Please come and try."

We all rushed toward the house and met Dan coming out of the woods chomping on the sickening red berries.

"Dan King! Do you want to commit suicide?" demanded the Story Girl.

"Look here, Dan. Are you crazy?" I said. "You shouldn't do this. Don't you remember how sick you were last night and all the trouble you made for everyone? Please don't eat any more."

"All right," said Dan. "I've eaten all I want. They taste fine. I don't believe it was them that made me sick anyway."

But now that his anger was over, he looked a little frightened. Felicity was not there. We found her in the kitchen, lighting up the fire.

"Bev, fill the kettle with water and put it on to heat," she said in a resigned tone. "If Dan's got to be sick again, we've got to be ready for it. I wish Mother was home, that's all. I hope she'll never go away again. Dan King, you just wait 'til I tell her the way you've acted."

"Fudge! I ain't gonna be sick," said Dan. "If you begin telling tales, Felicity King, *I'll* tell some, too.

I know how many eggs mother said you could use while she was away—and I know how many you have *used*. So you'd better mind your own business, Miss."

"A nice way to talk to your sister when you may be dead in an hour's time!" retorted Felicity. She was in tears now between her anger and real alarm about what could happen to Dan. "Why would you do such a stupid thing?" she moaned.

"I guess the devil made him do it," commented Peter.

In an hour's time, Dan was still in good health and said he was going to bed. He went and slept peacefully as if nothing was bothering his conscience or stomach. We wondered why he didn't get sick this time. The doctor had said the berries were poisonous.

"Maybe his system and stomach are used to them now," offered Felix by way of explanation.

Felicity declared that she meant to keep the water hot until all danger was past. We sat up to keep her company. We were still sitting there when Uncle Roger walked in at eleven o'clock.

"What on earth are you kids doing up at this time of night?" he stormed. "You should have been in your beds two hours ago. And with a roaring fire too on the hottest night of the summer. Are you all crazy?"

"It's because of Dan," explained Felicity wearily. "He went and ate more bad berries—a whole lot of them—and we were sure he'd be sick again. But he hasn't been yet, and now he's asleep."

"Is that boy stark raving mad?" questioned Uncle Roger. We could tell he had about had it with all of us.

"It was Felicity's fault," cried Cecily, once again taking Dan's part. "She told him she guessed he'd learned his lesson and would do what she told him the next time. He got so mad at her that he just went and ate 'em again."

"Felicity King, if you don't watch out, you'll grow up into the sort of woman who'll drive her husband to drink," said Uncle Roger seriously.

"How could I tell Dan would act like a mule?" said Felicity peevishly.

"Get off to bed, every one of you. I'll be very thankful when your father and mother come home. No bachelor should have to put up with a house full of children like you. Nobody will ever catch me doing it again. Felicity, is there anything fit to eat in the pantry?"

That was the most unkind thing Uncle Roger could have said to Felicity. She could have forgiven him for anything but that. She had really done a very good job of providing tasty meals and delicious desserts. She confided to me as we climbed the stairs that she hated Uncle Roger. Her red lips quivered and the tears of wounded pride brimmed in her beautiful blue eyes. In the dim candlelight, she looked so pretty and appealing. I put my arm around her and patted her encouragingly.

"Never mind him, Felicity," I said. "He's only a grown-up."

"I'm going to remember this when I'm a grown-up," said Cecily.

"I'm just awful tired," said the Story Girl. "It's hard work when you have to be a kid and a grown-up, too. I'll be glad when our grown-ups get back. It's *too* upsetting when they're away. That's my opinion."

"They'll be home tomorrow night," I said. "Not a minute too soon for me."

I think we all agreed as we trudged up to bed. It had been a fun adventure to "keep house" for a week, but lost babies and bad berries had taken their toll. Just now all that mattered was a good long sleep.

*Lucy Maud Montgomery*

1908

# Lucy Maud Montgomery
## 1874-1942

*Anne of Green Gables* was the very first book that Lucy Maud Montgomery published. In all, she wrote twenty-five books.

Lucy Maud Montgomery was born on Prince Edward Island. Her family called her Maud. Before she was two years old, her mother died and she was sent to live with her mother's parents on their farm on the Island. Her grandparents were elderly and very strict. Maud lived with them for a long time.

When she was seven, her father remarried. He moved far out west to Saskatchewan, Canada, with his new wife. At age seventeen, she went to live with them, but she did not get along with her stepmother. So she returned to her grandparents.

She attended college and studied to become a teacher—just like Anne in the Avonlea series. When her grandfather died, Maud went home to be with her grandmother. Living there in the quiet of Prince Edward Island, she had plenty of time to write. It was during this time that she wrote her first book, *Anne of Green Gables*. When the book was finally accepted, it was published soon after. It was an immediate hit, and Maud began to get thousands of letters asking for more stories about Anne. She wrote *Anne of Avonlea, Chronicles of Avonlea, Anne of the Island, Anne of Windy Poplars, Anne's House of Dreams, Rainbow Valley, Anne of Ingleside,* and *Rilla of Ingleside*. She also wrote *The Story Girl* and *The Golden Road*.

When Maud was thirty-seven years old, Ewan Macdonald, the minister of the local Presbyterian Church in Canvendish, proposed marriage to her. Maud accepted and they were married. Later on they moved to Ontario where two sons, Chester and Stewart, were born to the couple.

Maud never went back to Prince Edward Island to live again. But when she died in 1942, she was buried on the Island, near the house known as Green Gables.

Felix came tearing up the lane with a newspaper in his hand. When a boy as fat as Felix runs at full speed on a broiling August day, he has a good reason.

"He must have gotten some bad news at the post office," remarked Sara Ray.

"Oh, I hope nothing has happened to Father," I exclaimed, springing anxiously to my feet. I had a sick, horrible feeling of fear running over me like a cold, rippling wave.

"It's just as likely to be good news," said the Story Girl, who was always optimistic and liked to think the best.

"He wouldn't be running so fast for good news," said Dan.

We were not in doubt long. The orchard gate flew open, and Felix crashed through. As soon as we saw his face, we knew he wasn't bringing good news. He had been running hard, and for a boy his size, he should have been red-faced. Instead he was white as a sheet. I was in such fear that I couldn't even find my voice to ask him what was the matter. It was Felicity who impatiently demanded an explanation:

"Felix King, what has scared you?"

Felix held out the newspaper—it was the Charlottetown *Daily Enterprise*.

"It's there," he gasped. "Look ... read ... Oh, do you ... think ... it's true? The ... end ... of ... the world ... is coming tomorrow ... at two o'clock ... in the afternoon!"

Crash! Felicity had been drinking from the precious blue and white cup that had hung on the well in the orchard for generations. It had been there forever, it seemed. Now it lay shattered on the ground, but no one paid any attention. At any other time, we would have been horrified to have the blue well cup broken, but now it didn't matter to any of us. What did it matter if all the antique well cups in the world were broken today if the world was coming to an end?

"Oh Sara Stanley, do you believe it? *Do you?*" gasped Felicity, clutching the Story Girl's hand.

Cecily's prayer had been answered. In all the excitement, Felicity had spoken first. But this, like the breaking of the cup, had no significance for us at the moment.

The Story Girl snatched the paper and read the announcement to all of us who stood white, shaken, and silent—listening.

The headline read: "The Last Trump Will Sound at Two O'clock Tomorrow." The article had been written by a group in the United States that predicted August 12 would be Judgment Day. The article said the group's leader was encouraging group members to prepare for the end of the world by praying, fasting, and making white robes. It's funny to remember it now, but I will never forget the horror we felt in that sunny orchard that August morning. Keep in mind that we were only children and had a firm and simple faith that grown-ups knew far more than we did. We also believed that anything printed in a newspaper must be true.

"It can't be so," said Sara Ray, starting to cry as usual. "Do you believe it, Sara Stanley?"

"It *can't* be," said Felicity. "Everything looks just the same. Things can't look the same if Judgment Day is tomorrow."

"But that's just the way it is to come," I said, uncomfortable. "It says in the Bible that Judgment Day is to come like a thief in the night."

"But it also says in the Bible that nobody knows when the Judgment Day is to come—not even the angels in heaven," said Cecily eagerly. "Do you suppose the editor of the *Enterprise* knows something the angels in heaven don't even know? He's just a Grit [a Democrat], you know."

"I guess he knows as much about it as a Tory would," retorted the Story Girl. Uncle Roger's political persuasion was liberal, and Uncle Alec was a conservative. We cousins always argued for the political party of the older people who were the heads of our households.

"But it isn't really the *Enterprise* newspaper editor who is saying it," continued the Story Girl. "It's a man in the United States who claims to be a prophet. If he truly *is* a prophet, maybe he knows more than we do here in Canada."

"And it's in the newspaper too, in print just like the Bible," said Dan.

"Well, I'm going to depend on the Bible," said Cecily. "I don't believe it's the Judgment Day tomorrow—but I'm scared anyway."

That was exactly how we all felt. Just like the bell-ringing ghost, we didn't think it could be, but we were still afraid.

"I don't know," said Dan doubtfully. "The Bible was printed thousands of years ago, and that

paper was printed this morning. It's more up-to-date."

"Yeah, but the Bible has been around for so long, it has to be true," remarked Felix.

"I want to do so many things," said the Story Girl. "But if it's the Judgment Day tomorrow, I won't have time to do any of them."

"It can't be much worse than dying, I s'pose," said Felix. He was grasping at anything that might bring him comfort.

"I'm awful glad I've got into the habit of going to church and Sunday school this summer," said Peter soberly. "I wish I'd made up my mind before this whether to be a Presbyterian or a Methodist. Do you s'pose it's too late now?"

"Oh, that doesn't matter," said Cecily earnestly. "If—if you're a Christian, Peter, that is all that's necessary."

"But it's too late for that," said Peter miserably. "I can't turn into a Christian between now and two o'clock tomorrow. I'll just have to be satisfied with making up my mind to be a Presbyterian or a Methodist. I wanted to wait 'til I got old enough to make out what was the difference, but I'll have to chance it now. I guess I'll be a Presbyterian, 'cause I want to be like the rest of you. Yes, I'll be a Presbyterian."

"I know a story about Judy Pineau and the word 'Presbyterian,'" said the Story Girl, "but I can't tell it now. If tomorrow isn't the Judgment Day, I'll tell it Monday."

"If I had known that tomorrow might be the Judgment Day, I wouldn't have quarreled with you last Monday, Sara Stanley, or been so horrid and sulky all week. Indeed, I wouldn't have," said Felicity, with unusual humility.

Felicity not only had spoken first, but here was a bit of an apology. So many amazing things were running through our heads, the things we would have done differently, "if we had only known." A black list of sins—an endless list—rushed through all of our young memories. For us the Book of Judgment was already open, and there we stood with no defense.

I thought of all the bad things I had done in my lifetime. I thought of when I had pinched Felix to make him cry out at family prayers, when I had played hooky from Sunday school and went fishing instead, and of a big fib—no, let's call it like it was— a big *lie*—I had told. I feared that the next day I might have to answer for all of them. Oh, how I wished I'd been a better boy!

Everyone else was thinking seriously too. "The quarrel was as much my fault as yours, Felicity," said

the Story Girl, putting her arm around her friend. "We can't undo it now. But if tomorrow isn't the Judgment Day, we must be careful never to quarrel again."

"Oh, I wish my father were here," she continued. "I wonder if it is the Judgment Day in Europe where he is? Do you suppose I'll ever see him again?" she worried.

"You will," assured Cecily, who seemed to be our religious authority. "If it is the Judgment Day for Prince Edward Island, it will be for Europe and the whole world."

"I just wish we *knew*," said Felix desperately. "I'd do a whole lot better if I just knew."

Whom could we ask? Uncle Alec, our most trusted confidant, was away and would not be back until late that night. We didn't want to ask Aunt Janet nor Uncle Roger—worried that they would laugh and scoff at us. We were afraid of the Judgment Day, but we were also afraid of being laughed at.

"How about Aunt Olivia?" I asked.

"No, Aunt Olivia has gone to bed with a sick headache and mustn't be disturbed," said the Story Girl. "Besides, what good would it do to ask the grown-ups? They don't know anything more about this than we do."

"But if they'd just say they didn't believe it, it would be sort of a comfort," said Cecily.

"I suppose the minister would know, but he's away on vacation," said Felicity. "Anyhow, I'll go and ask Mother what she thinks of it."

Felicity picked up the newspaper and headed for the house. We waited in agony for her return.

"Well, what did she say?" demanded Cecily when Felicity returned.

"She said, 'Run away and don't bother me. I don't have time for any of your nonsense,'" Felicity said in an injured tone. "When I said, 'The paper says tomorrow,' Ma just said, 'Judgment; Fiddlesticks!'"

"We'll just have to ask Uncle Roger," said Felix finally. This was definitely our last resort and our willingness to risk his ridicule showed how really desperate we were.

Uncle Roger was in the barnyard hitching his black mare to his buggy. His copy of the *Enterprise* newspaper was sticking out of his back pocket. We saw with sinking hearts that he seemed unusually sad. There was not a glimmer of a smile on his face.

"You ask him," said Felicity, nudging the Story Girl.

# *The King Cousins*
## (Book 1)
## By L.M. Montgomery,
## Adapted by Barbara Davoll

Sara Stanley, the Story Girl, can captivate anyone who will listen to her tales. In this first book of the series, brothers Beverley and Felix arrive on Prince Edward Island to spend the summer with their cousins on the King homestead. These curious and imaginative children set out to investigate the existence of God.

S<small>OFTCOVER</small> 0-310-70598-3

*Available now at your local bookstore!*

# Zonder**kidz**.

# *Summer Shenanigans*
## (Book 3)
## By L.M. Montgomery, Adapted
## by Barbara Davoll

The King cousins read a dreaded prophecy about Judgment Day. When they hear a mysterious, ghostly ringing bell, they are frightened nearly out of their wits, thinking it has something to do with the end of the world. They become so frightened that the Story Girl refuses to tell any more stories. This book is filled with shenanigans and rollicking summer days as the King cousins try to make the most of their time together on Prince Edward Island.

SOFTCOVER 0-310-70600-9

*Available now at your local bookstore!*

# Zonderkidz.

We want to hear from you. Please send your
comments about this book to us in care of
zreview@zondervan.com.
Thank you.

# Zonder**kidz**®

*Grand Rapids, MI 49530*
www.zonderkidz.com